Nikita Sataram

Pride Of Bloodlines

Nikita Sataram

Pride Of Bloodlines

There is no Hell

JustFiction Edition

Impressum/Imprint (nur für Deutschland/only for Germany)
Bibliografische Information der Deutschen Nationalbibliothek: Die Deutsche
Nationalbibliothek verzeichnet diese Publikation in der Deutschen Nationalbibliografie;
detaillierte bibliografische Daten sind im Internet über http://dnb.d-nb.de abrufbar.
Alle in diesem Buch genannten Marken und Produktnamen unterliegen warenzeichen-,
marken- oder patentrechtlichem Schutz bzw. sind Warenzeichen oder eingetragene
Warenzeichen der jeweiligen Inhaber. Die Wiedergabe von Marken, Produktnamen,
Gebrauchsnamen, Handelsnamen, Warenbezeichnungen u.s.w. in diesem Werk berechtigt
auch ohne besondere Kennzeichnung nicht zu der Annahme, dass solche Namen im Sinne
der Warenzeichen- und Markenschutzgesetzgebung als frei zu betrachten wären und
daher von jedermann benutzt werden dürften.

Coverbild: www.ingimage.com

Verlag: JustFiction! Edition ist ein Imprint der
LAP LAMBERT Academic Publishing GmbH & Co. KG
Heinrich-Böcking-Str. 6-8, 66121 Saarbrücken, Deutschland
Telefon +49 681 37 20 310, Telefax +49 681 37 20 310-9
Email: info@justfiction-edition.com

Herstellung in Deutschland:
Schaltungsdienst Lange o.H.G., Berlin
Books on Demand GmbH, Norderstedt
Reha GmbH, Saarbrücken
Amazon Distribution GmbH, Leipzig
ISBN: 978-3-8454-4525-0

Imprint (only for USA, GB)
Bibliographic information published by the Deutsche Nationalbibliothek: The Deutsche
Nationalbibliothek lists this publication in the Deutsche Nationalbibliografie; detailed
bibliographic data are available in the Internet at http://dnb.d-nb.de.
Any brand names and product names mentioned in this book are subject to trademark,
brand or patent protection and are trademarks or registered trademarks of their respective
holders. The use of brand names, product names, common names, trade names, product
descriptions etc. even without a particular marking in this works is in no way to be
construed to mean that such names may be regarded as unrestricted in respect of
trademark and brand protection legislation and could thus be used by anyone.

Cover image: www.ingimage.com

Publisher: JustFiction! Edition
is an imprint of the publishing house
LAP LAMBERT Academic Publishing GmbH & Co. KG
Heinrich-Böcking-Str. 6-8, 66121 Saarbrücken, Germany
Phone +49 681 37 20 310, Fax +49 681 37 20 310-9
Email: info@justfiction-edition.com

Printed in the U.S.A.
Printed in the U.K. by (see last page)
ISBN: 978-3-8454-4525-0

For my little sister Deeya, thank you for always being there for me
-Love Kita-

<u>Chapter 1</u>

Isolated from humanity bathed in a thick mist and hidden from the eyes of our enemies for many centuries, a true sanctuary for my people the same people you have treat like filth for many lifetimes.
I am Anastasia Scarlet King, the eldest daughter of Ariana and Darien Scarlet King, my parents.

Midnight black hair and deep brown eyes and lightly tanned skin. Sounds about right for an 18 year old, well I think so anyway, partly because that is me. I am Anastasia.

I'm a twin, and my brothers name is Krish.
But after us were born our 6 other siblings 3 boys and 3 girls, 2 of them are twin boys Odion and Max; both 2 years younger than us black hair like mother and green eyes like our father.
Mina and Charlotte were the youngest of the clan, aged 5 and 6 and before them, Ryan and Anaie; ages 15 and 12.

Indeed we have a big family, but I know I wouldn't have it any other way, since family is all we have left in this world.
Mind you...that wasn't the case 300 years ago.
By now I'm sure you've picked up on this...I'm not "human", and I'm ashamed to have to say that.

My family and I live in a fair size village in the middle of an ancient forest outside London. No one dares to set foot inside, they know something is lurking within, and once you get in, getting out won't be so easy.

However all those years ago this wasn't the case, humans did come in, they would scout around and the few that made it to the Village and that did know about us...forever remained the few.

Krish and I have had our fair share of blood in our lives; in fact it was one evening many years ago when we were walking within the surrounding forest.

Fog had surrounded the forest and as we were walking and talking we heard noises. We stopped and focused on the sounds; we could hear footsteps and could smell fresh flowing blood.
We both leapt into the trees keeping our eyes on the ground. Not long after we saw 2 men walking along, then past us.
I looked up at my brother and smiled as my eyes gleamed, he knew what I was thinking.

I tightly gripped the rope I had wound around my waist; we nodded to each other and then went separate ways.

He went ahead of them and I followed behind, I heard rustling from the trees and bushes; Krish was on the move. I then heard gasps coming from the humans spinning around trying to find what was causing the sounds.

I proceeded closer and knelt down, I could faintly see their bodies in the fog, I licked my lips and then with a crack I let loose my rope around their legs drawing them harshly together; then jumping up and have them hanging upside down.
I pulled tighter and ensured they wouldn't move.
I then jumped down and met with Krish who was lightly laughing, we slapped our palms together then turned to our captives.

"Well, well Anastasia what do we have here?" he asked mockingly.
"Well Krish, two trespassers I think, but you know what brother?" I responded in the same tone.
"No, what?" he responded
"I hate trespassers!" I spat out.
"As do I Ana, as do I"
"Unhand us you demons!" one man exclaimed.

An old man with grey hair, weak blue eyes and coloured flesh
"You walk into our domain….and want us to let you go?" My brother asked in a mono toned voice.

"That's some demand dear brother, even then…they came armed" I spoke as I bent down and picked up two axes.

Krish took the axes from me and threw one at a nearby tree digging in a good few inches deep inside.
"God will punish you both, you children of the Devil!" screamed out the other man, who was rather good-looking lovely green eyes and rather stunning blonde hair.

I then knelt down and licked his cheek, "hmm, your God has no power over Hell"
"Hell is where you were born!" shouted the young man.

I then stood up and circled around them, and Krish did the same the other direction.
"Then so are you, because this is Hell, there may be a heaven but there is no earth"
"They are both one and the same" we said in unison.
"You creatures are wrong!" the old man screamed

"Oh tell it to your God!" I said then turned away as high-pitched, violent wild screams of pain and anguish could be heard echoing around the forest.

Krish had used the second axe and hacked away at their bodies, digging harshly into their skins and making them remain forever silent.

I then turned to the blooded bodies and slid my fingers across the young man's face and licked the blood off.
"Hmm not bad, needs to be sweeter" I said as I licked my lips.
"You have too much of a sweet tooth as far as I'm concerned; that's sweet enough for you young lady" he responded firmly.

I then glared at him and then we both made our way back home.
Krish and I are very close and always have been, the link between us is quite powerful; especially our mental link. Most of the time we could almost read each other's thoughts

Well I think I should explain to you a bit more about our village. Our clan is one of few that is scattered around the world, from Elegant England to Active America; however our race is dwindling, or so I'm told.

An ancient race of dark creatures with amazing power, a truly supreme race-again as I was told to think, I did believe it, but I longed too much for everything that humans had that I even began to hate them; it is because of humans that we are the way we are...but more about that another time.

My brother Krish does agree with me but isn't as furious or passionate as I am about the matter. As for my parents, well; they are the leaders of our clan.

Arlana, my mother one of the most beautiful women in the village, and my father Darien the most ignorant man I have ever met; but yet is a strong leader and has managed to keep us alive this long.

But together, they along with all the other clan leaders around the world, thrive for one thing; the survival of our race.

Our village is very secluded from outsiders and we always keep to ourselves, however there are the odd few times in which people like Zack and Dylan, would go to the outside world and bring fresh blood for the village; 2-3 people a month.

Ray, Hayden, Zack and Dylan the few younger men of the village; however their cocky attitude fails them a lot of the time.

Ray's parents and mine have been pushing him and me to get together for years. I've been brought up to respect my elders but- they must be bloody mad!
I can't imagine being with him, mind you that's never stopped him and his flirtatious behaviour.

And if it's not him it's his little sister Laura, always hanging around my brother like a bad stink. She would always try her best to get with any man in our village but all turned her down, just as well if you ask me.

That entirely aside I'm sure you can see we have our own issues within our village, but none of this fairly peaceful life will ever remain the same.

Mariana the elder of our village, and she is said to have the ability to see into the future; she was sent to us from Romania to help guide us through our eternal life.
And not that many days ago she had told me that a great disaster would devastate our village and many important ones would be lost.

Mother however told me that no such thing would happen and that there is nothing to worry about; but I couldn't help but feel it could be true, her words always passes through my mind and her serious voice echoed in my ear.
Even Krish felt the same way I did, but he couldn't help but agree with mother, but time would tell and that's all there is to it.

It's a new day and by that I mean another day of survival, however now that I think about it there have been no attacks or raids on our village for years; not that I'm complaining because what peace we have, we enjoy.
In fact I remember an attack that was launched at us, my life was changed that day.

It was a late summer night, Krish and I we were settled into bed. He was sound asleep, but not me; I lay there wide awake and bored.
So I got out of bed and made my way to the window, sighing I looked around at the outside.

Suddenly I heard a faint shouting...and screaming and the flicker of lights. I opened the window wide letting a gust of autumn wind blow in, I jumped out and made a run around the house to the front. There I saw my parents and a group of the rest of the villagers running after these 3 men with daggers and pitchforks.
Humans. They had found their way in, but they would never find a way out.

I then made my way back to my bedroom window but stopped when I heard someone come up behind me.

I spun around and saw a man holding a silver cross to me; I jumped back pressing my body against the wall.
"Die you child of the Devil!" he screamed.
I began to feel weak and fell to my knees hoping that my supposing eternal life wouldn't end soon.
I close my eyes and waited; a sudden scream and then saw the human tossed a good few feet away from me. I then saw Uncle Gareth standing before me.
"Run Ana! Get back inside" he demanded

I went to do so but as I put my second leg through the window I heard a scream of pain and anguish. I turned to see my uncle with a steak stabbed through his heart.

I screamed and saw the human heading for me but suddenly stopped half way and fell face forward to the ground, there I saw my father standing with a blood covered dagger in his hand. He ran over and tightly hugged me.

"Are you alright Anastasia?" he asked and kissed the top of my head.
"I am ok father" I lightly gasped.

We both then turned to Uncle Gareth who lay there breathing deeply and rapidly. Father ran over to him and held up his head.

"Brother, speak to me!" my father wailed.
"Looks as if I won't be lasting too long" he faintly spoke.
"Do not worry you'll be fine" my father said, trying to speak hopefully.

I had again jumped out the window and was standing next to my father, looking at my uncle as a tear slid down my cheek.

"I...I'm sorry uncle, it's my fault" I lightly sobbed.
"No Ana, don't blame yourself, besides it is best that you're safe" he gasped out.

"But you will be alright" I said trying to sound as hopeful as my father.
"I think not...the...steak is piercing my heart, one m...move and I will die, I...I'm faintly surviving" even he filled up with tears now.

"Oh dear" said a voice.
I turned to see Krish.
"Uncle Gareth..." he said
"Hi there Lad, d...do not worry about me, j...just help your sister and father, the c...clan will look t...to you for leadership"
Krish rested a hand on my shoulder

"I promise Uncle" he lightly whimpered.

Uncle Gareth slightly moved and within seconds, his body remained
forever still and turned into dust in my father's arms.
I turned and cried into Krish's shoulder as he tightly wrapped his arms
around me.

Father stood up and firmly brushed his hand over his head. Suddenly then
mother came running over and gasped covering her mouth in horror.
"O...oh goodness" she said.
"D...Devils!" we heard being shouted. We saw the human that killed my
uncle trying to stand up.
"M...may you s...suffer dearly when you die, f...for God cares not f...for
Demons like you!"

I looked at the floor and saw the dagger my father used, still with fresh
glistening blood on it.
I rapidly picked it up and with my swift speed I stood behind the man.

"Then go and be with your God!" I shouted as I swiftly slit the dagger
clear across his throat.
He screamed in pure pain and anguish as I left him to bleed on the grass.
"Ana-"started Krish.
"I DON'T CARE! HE KILLED FAMILY! HE DESERVED IT!" I screamed at him
and threw the dagger into the humans back and stormed into the forest.

My first taste of violence...and I loved it.
The feeling was incredible knowing that their "God" was not the only one
that can take life away.
He deserved it and I was more than glad to be the one to do it.
I looked down at my hands and saw his crimson blood streaming down
past my wrists; my eyes gleamed with lust as I licked it clean off my hand.
I sighed then cleaned the rest off on a tree; I then began to make my
way back to the village.

A rather exciting day in my life, and it my first kill.
However I have never forgiven myself for what happened that day. If I
had not come out of my room, my uncle would still be alive today.

Which is why from that day, I have showed no mercy to any human. We
never kill more than our feed 3 people a month, and only more if they
came wondering in. But those who wish to kill us...suffer very dearly.

I'm sure you can now see how the past has had a great influence on me.
But now in the present things are very different. It's much quieter; hardly
anyone comes in...so we have to send a few out to get some.

None the less it's a new day now and as usual nothing to do. Father
doesn't let anyone leave unless it's for food.
However even if we don't get people for our food, we tend to feed off the
animals in the forest; but we try not to so much just so that they can
breed more.

I really enjoy being in the village so I tend to wonder around the forest.

As per usual nothing much to do, I've been around here so long that I
have no idea what year it is, mind you not that I care...but I would like to
know what those lowlife species have been up to all these years.

<u>**Chapter 2**</u>

Another boring day in my boring life. My name is Lee, your typical 18 year old, blonde hair, blue eyed good looking lad.
And no I'm not cocky just…confident.
I do well in school and have lots of mates, a girlfriend and a rich family.
So I guess you could say I live quite a high life.

Anyway a typical Friday night, just came back from a house party and of course dead tired, went up to my room and quickly had a shower and rested on my bed.

"God I'm so bloody tired" I sighed as I closed my eyes.
"Lee get down here this instant!" screamed my mother.

My eyes snapped open and I groaned as I went out my room and made my way downstairs.
I walked down the faintly lit hallway until I got to the main living room, which is where my mother is most of the time.
Rolling my eyes I knocked on the door.

"Come in" she yelled from inside.

So in I went and closed the door behind me, and sitting in the red velvet sofa was my mother. Alison Katy V.Hsing.
I had her stunning blue eyes but my dads' hair; at least it's what I've been told by my mother.
Dad was said to have passed away before I was born, in a war or something, so I never knew him.

"Lee, Gabriel V.Hsing come here and say hello to your Great Grandfather" she said.

I felt like slapping myself for forgetting he was coming. The most important people in the family, for his wisdom, knowledge and his supposing escape of death.
I don't think I got told the story; apparently I was too young to know what happened.

Great Grandfather was over 90 years old but looked more like 60 than anything else.
I walked over and extended my hand to him and he firmly shook mine.

"Welcome Great Grandpa" I said respectfully.
"Dear Lee, you look more and more like your father Gabriel every time I see you" he softly spoke.

Although I never met my father, I was still told that he was a great man who passed on by committing a great sacrifice. Or that's what I have been told.
"Sit down Hun" mum said.

So I did and sighed resting back onto the sofa, she then stood up and went to start up the fire.
"How is school going Gabriel?" asked my grandpa.

He always called me by that name and not just because it was my middle name but because it reminded him of my father, his grandson.
"Very well thanks, I'm doing P.E, History and French" I responded.

He smiled but said nothing, followed by an odd silence; which was then broken by a familiar ringing that came from my mothers' phone.

"Excuse me" she said.
"Hello, yes…oh hello, I'm fine thank you- yourself? Oh how lovely, oh yes tomorrow…oh well- actually that will be fine; ok see you there" thus ends her conversation.

"Who was that mum?" I curiously asked.
"John from work, there's a meeting tomorrow afternoon; and I'm required to go" she responded.

"And I am going which means you have to take your grandfather to the Crimson table, his favourite restaurant"
"But I-"
"No 'buts' young man, you came in late today so you're taking him out tomorrow" she spoke sternly.

I sighed knowing arguing with her was pointless, and just nodded.
"Now off to bed, you have a busy day tomorrow"
"Ok…goodnight, sleep well Grandfather"

I slightly bowed my head and made my way back upstairs.
Once back in my room I lay in bed slightly annoyed.

"Guess going to the park and lunch with the lads is out of the question, oh well"
With that I turned out my sidelight and slowly drifted off to sleep.

Sunrise and I was already awake. So after getting myself dressed and making my bed I grabbed my laptop and headed to the kitchen, and there was mum having her usual cup of tea in her chair at the table.
"Morning dear, sleep well?"

"Yeah, I guess so, what's there to eat?" I asked
"There's pancake mix next to the stove, make one" she responded.

As I was making my food she had left the kitchen and came back by the time I finished cooking it.

"Here, there's about £30.00, use it to pay for your day out" she said.
I nodded then sat down at the table and started eating.
"Ok, well I'm going to get ready I have food shopping to do before the meeting"

She then headed out of the kitchen back upstairs. I sighed and carried on eating; once I was done I just sat there and let my mind wonder.
Not long into my day dreaming did my Grandpa walk in smiling at me.

"Morning Gabriel" he cheerfully said.
"Morning grandpa, sleep well" I asked
"Very well my lad, I always do when I come here" he responded
"Want some pancakes?"
"No thank you my lad, but a cup of tea would be nice" he asked.

I nodded and went to put the kettle on, then got out a cup and dropped in a tea bag, no sugar and whole milk, just the way he likes it.

Grandpa always came over when he could and we enjoyed having him around, he was always a good laugh and told the most fascinating stories; some rather horrific and scary, but I was told those kind of stories from when I was 12.
It was strange because the way he told it was as if he was there.

So much detail and emotions were put into the description and feelings of the characters; they were so raw and allowed you to get into their minds.

I remember one story always gave me chills.
He called it "Demons of the forest".
I can just about remember it, but not in great detail; partly because it had been years since I was told the story.

But I always remembered one part, and that bit always echoed in my mind. The ending, where one of two men in the forest was caught, he fought valiantly but as he did he was attacked by another creature with his last force of strength, screamed for the second man to run for his life.

Despite showing how reluctant he was he made a run down the dark path out of the woods, leaving his friend to suffer at the hands of those demonic creatures.

"Gabriel are you alright lad?" said a voice.

"Huh? Oh, yes I'm fine, just thinking" I responded rather slowly.
I then quickly gave him his tea and headed upstairs.

Once in my room I closed the door and went outside on the balcony.
There I looked down at the town as the sun rose and covered everything
in its golden light.

Chapter 3

Finally night had fallen and tonight the boys would be heading out for
some fresh blood.
Zack and Dylan would be the ones hunting outside the forest this evening.
Two of the youngest and most ruthless hunters, both aged 19 and very
quick to the job.

Zack was the more violent lad who preferred offence to defence. Stunning
black hair, emerald eyes and moon pale skin.

Dylan, one of the "pretty boys" of the Village, lush brown hair, hazel eyes
and again moon pale skin.

Certainly had more of a tactical approach to his work than Zack, which is
why they made a good team.

Hopefully today they can bring back some perfectly aged blood.
As for me, I'm currently in my room enjoying the darkness that had
surrounded our village, but I could not relax. I couldn't help but once
again let my mind wonder about how I ended up the way me everyone in
the village became the way we are.

Chapter 4

As I was almost forced to do I took grandpa out to dinner, after paying a meal worth about thirty pounds we began to head home.

Mum had borrowed the car so we'd have to take a taxi home.
So we began to make our way to the main town where all the taxies were parked.

"Let's cut across the park" I suggested, "It will take less time to get into town that way"
"You sure it's safe Gabriel?" he said slightly unsure.

"Oh come on, what could go wrong?" I said
Which was true, nothing really goes on in that park; so it is pretty much safe.
Seriously what is the worst that would happen in this town?

So we crossed the road and made our way down the path that wound through the park.
The moonlight beautifully lit the park, especially reflecting off the water in the fountain.
As we walked through enjoying the surrounding we suddenly heard rustling from the trees and bushes.

"What was that?" stuttered Grandpa
"Just the wind" I swiftly answered.

It wasn't even that strong, but I don't see why he worried so much, I'd protect him.
Or so I thought anyway.
Suddenly from out of the darkness of the trees someone jumped out and tackled me to the floor.

"Got you boy!" said the shadowed figure.
Without even thinking I punched the guy in the chest sending him flying off me.
He had landed on his back but sprung back up onto his feet.

"Guess you're not coming quietly are you" he snarled.
Next thing I knew the guy came charging at me!
But within a flash the guy just suddenly disappeared.

"Shit...where is he?!" I gasped
A sudden kick from behind into my back caused me to fall onto my front; I turned back around but saw no one again.

I turned to Grandpa who was still where I left him just looking around panicked like I was.

"What's going on?!" I screamed.

No sound or movement from around us. I quickly stood up and ran over to him.
"Let's go"
But before going any further I was gripped tightly by the shoulders and thrown back onto one of the park benches.

As I sat there in slight pain that guy I was fighting appeared in front of me, with the moons beams now on him; I could see him more clearly.
A very young man; brown haired, green eyed and moon pale skin.

"Gabriel catch!" I hear from my Grandfather.
With that I had something silver thrown at me, I held it up and I saw a small cross.
The guy jumped back and hissed; as he did...I could have sworn I saw fangs. He then retreated and made a run for it.

My Grandpa then ran over to me as I was in a moment of shock.
"Gabriel, come on let's leave now!" he urged.
So with that we quickly made out way to town.

Once there we got a taxi back home. On the way we were both silent, what was there to say?
I mean did what just happen really happen? Or have I read or seen too many bad vampire movies and books.
Not too long in the taxi had we arrived home, in we both went closing and locking the door behind us.

Grandpa then walked with me to the main living room and we both sat down.

"Grandpa, w...what happened?" I stuttered in shock.
"I didn't think they came out of the forest, guess I was wrong" he spoke in a light voice.

"Grandpa please...I think you know something about this" I said.
"Indeed Gabriel, I do" He sighed.

He then sat next to me and sighed again.
"I suppose considering the family history, you should know"
"Family...history?" I was getting more confused by all this now.

"Do you remember the stories I used to tell you years ago?" he asked.
I slowly nodded my head.

"Well there was a story that I told you about two men that went into the forest not far from here, I'm sorry to say it was a true story" still confused I said nothing.

"It started many years ago, there were two men wondering around the forest in search of a hidden Village of creatures that lurked within. These creatures were able to take the life of others and natural enemies of light" he started.

"It was a late on an August evening and the two men entered the forest and continued walking in until they soon came to an old village" He continued.

"On they went, and as they did they could see the sun was setting and oddly quite fast. One asked the other if they should leave. But he refused and said 'Our bloodline depends on us to carry out this task. We may not get them all, but even one is good enough to lower the lower the number of these demons'. Just as he said that candle lightly flickered on around the village"

Grandpa's story was becoming more and more familiar to me, memories of this story were flooding my mind, and the mental images of that village haunted my thoughts.

"G...go on" I stuttered.
Grandpa sighed then took a deep breath to carry on his story.

"After the candles came on, they heard doors being unlocked and opened, so they ran and hid around side of a small hut where no one could see them" I leaned slightly forward as the story pulled me in further.

"They remained calm and still. For if their heart rate was to increase...the demons would hear their rapid pulse. They then glanced at each other and carefully peered around the corner and were surprised at what they saw. Dozens of men, women and children around everywhere, but lad, there is something you must know; these were not normal people you are used to...they are as in-human as the creatures that attacked us. Gabriel they were Vampires"

To be honest, years ago I thought nothing of this because... I always thought of it just to be a story to scare and entertain me.
But because he told me before he started this story that this was all true...made me now think it was all rubbish.

"Grandpa-", I started.
"Gabriel it's true, I swear on your father's grave that it's true!"
"You expect me to believe that rubbish?!" I yelled back at him.
"You have to! For the power of destroying these creatures' runs through your veins!" he screamed back at me.

<u>Chapter 5</u>

Hours had passed since Zack and Dylan had left to get food, which was odd because usually there would come back 30 minutes after leaving.

And since they've been gone so long, my hunger level has increased, I'm yearning for fresh blood and soft flesh.

Sick of waiting I left my room and made my way downstairs, so I proceeded outside and sat on the railing that ran around the porch outside the house.

I looked up into the night sky and sighed at the diamond stars that glistened above; a light sigh and I closed my eyes.

"And what are you sighing about?" I heard two voices say.

I didn't even have to open my eyes to know who it was, Odion and Max; real monsters of the Clan.

"What do you both want?" I groaned.
"Awww, maybe she's in love brother" Odion teased.
"Maybe she is" added Max.

Standing up from the step I looked down at them.
"Haven't you village fools got anything better to do?" I asked

"No, not at the moment" they said in unison then followed up with two cheeky smiles.

I rolled my eyes and walked past them and began to make my way to the meeting hall, hopefully my parents would still be there.

As I was walking through the more residential part of the village, I then felt a whip of wind fly past me.

"Alright Ray, come out" I sighed.
"Oh, how'd you know it was me?" He groaned.

He jumped down from the large Oak tree landing on one knee and foot, and then slowly stood up.

As he did, the candles around the village revealed his stunning features; icy blue eyes and blonde hair all complimented by his smooth tanned skin.

Pretty much a typical pretty boy, and the one every girl and woman would dream of having for a mate.

Despite his looks I must say the boy does not appeal to me.

"No one else rushes past me like you do, or rather no one does…just you-stalker" I responded.

He stood up straight with his arms folded.
"You should be flattered then, you should also know that I don't go after just anyone" he boasted.

"Am I supposed to be flattered by that?"
I sighed and rolled my eyes then turned away from him.

"Excuse me, I have to see my parents"
However before proceeding any further I was stopped by a tight grip around on my right wrist. Turning around I saw it was Ray.

"Ana, don't you think it's that point in life where the clan should be expanded? Admit it, you know for a fact that we could take your parents place; this clan could bring our race to its former glory that it was hundreds of years ago" he explained.

He sounded like he was lecturing me, and worse he sounded like both our parents.

I simply pulled my wrist away.

"Don't start Ray, I have no interest in bothering with this now, there is more than enough time…for me to pick a decent partner anyway"
With that I carried on my way to the Hall.

<u>**Chapter 6**</u>

I sat there, frozen, and confused "Power"?
What was he saying; maybe the old man finally lost it.

"Gabriel, I'm serious boy and now is better than ever to know how far and where your bloodline leads to" my Grandpa explained.

He then stood up and made his way to the far right of our almost endless bookcase; he pulled out a crimson book and placed it on the coffee table.

"My Lad, I think you should finally learn about your noble bloodline" he said.

With that he opened the book at the first page. There was an old piece of paper and what appeared to be a Polaroid picture.
He picked it up and showed it to me.

"This is me and your father, before we went into the forest, you see Lad, those two men in the story…were me and your father; I regret that it all happened while your mother was giving birth to you" he explained.

For a moment there I had to stop breathing, just thinking about what I was told, my father…died because of some creatures that I had thought were made up.

I quickly breathed in and out.

"Grandpa, this is ridiculous; mother said he died in a battle, not fighting some creatures of fantasy" I responded slightly raising my voice.

"Gabriel-"he started.
"No, I've had enough for this evening"

With that I just left him and went straight to my room.
I took my jacket off and threw it on my chair then fell back on my bed;
my thoughts being flooded by Grandpa's words;
Vampires, my "powers"…my father.

I closed my eyes and let the thoughts run through my head.
Eventually I felt myself drifting off, however all the silence of my thoughts were broken by my phone ringing loudly.

Annoyed, I opened my eyes and leaned over to my chair pulling my coat towards me then reaching in my pocket for my phone.
Not bothering to check who it was I answered.

"Hello?" I said with as little enthusiasm as possible.

"Well, don't sound too happy" said a voice.
And whose I knew all too well; Jenifer, my girlfriend, who I had been devoting my heart to for over 3 years.

"Hi Jen, sorry, took my grandfather out this evening, so I'm quite tired" I explained.

"Aww, that's ok Hun, anyway think you'll be up for our dinner tomorrow?" she asked sweetly.

I sighed then took a slight breath.

"Sure Jen, I'd like that"
"Good, pick me up at 8" she said in her peppy voice.
"Cool, night love" I sleepily said.
"Night hunny" she responded.

We both cut the phone and I placed it on my side table.
I couldn't even find the will to get dressed so I pulled back my covers and tucked into my bed, trying to push everything out of my head.

Chapter 7

Taking only several steps forward did I sniff and smell fresh blood.

"Dinners ready!" shouted a voice.
Zack and Dylan were back.

So I thought I would see mother and father later.
With that I sped off to the village centre, there were 3 bodies lying there all with different wounds on them.

One with a deep gash in the neck, another with several stab wounds and the last one with a deep gash cut down their chest.

"Hi there Ana" I turned around to meet with Dylan.
"Hi how was the hunt today?" I asked.
"Well it was-"
"Shit!" screamed a voice.

I turned back to the bodies and saw Zack standing there.
"Aww what went wrong?" I asked in a babyish voice.
"Nothing!" Zack exclaimed.
Obviously a lie.

"Oh he's just mad about how two humans for away earlier" Dylan explained.
"So…" I started.
"No one gets away from me! Bad enough it was a teen and an old man!" he screamed.

"His pride is injured" added Dylan as he rolled his eyes.
"Ok well you have my sympathy, can we eat now?" I said
"You've got a heart of gold Ana" Zack said sarcastically.

Just then the villagers all began to gather around to feast.
All thirty eight children of the village were present they would get one body among themselves then the remaining two would be for the remainder.

Two glasses per person was enough to last us another month, as for what's left (if any) it's stored in bottles/jars and kept in the supply cabin.

Normally if we had a lot in the cabin we wouldn't have to hunt, but we are low on blood and we were becoming more lustful for it.
It would be rare when we would need more than three a month.

Time had passed this evening and it was now that point where we all would be preparing for our rest.

However, one thing had been nagging at the back of my mind since the feast. What exactly happened between Zack and the humans that escaped, despite not showing much interest earlier because I was hungry; I wanted to know.

So I made my way to the large Oak tree in the middle of the village, and there as usual; were Zack and Dylan.

"Hi Lads" I said.
Zack was sitting up in the tree; he looked down at me and sighed.

"And what do you want?" he asked, clearly still not happy.
"Just curious; so, what did happen on the hunt earlier?" I asked.
"Please Anastasia, like you really give a damn" he spat out.

"Come on Zack, she's just asking" Dylan said, trying to reason with him.
"Please, I would really like to know" I said more eager now.
"Fine then little Miss nosey" he finally agreed.

<u>Chapter 8</u>

Morning was here now. I slowly sat up in bed feeling refreshed, until words and images of last night washed into my mind again.

"Oh God" I sighed as I firmly brushed my hand through my hair.

I managed to pull myself out of bed and get ready.
Once I was done I made my way downstairs, I didn't even bother eating breakfast; lost my appetite.
So I went into the back living room and fell back onto the sofa.

I sighed and closed my eyes and breathed in the sweet cinnamon smell that floated around the room.

However my thoughts were interrupted by a text message from my phone.
I pulled it out of my pocket and saw it was from Jen.

"Don't forget, we have dinner tonight; pick me up at 8. Love you" I read aloud.

Something like this should help put my mind at ease, or at least I hope so.
I stood up and made my way to the hall, just as I walked into it I saw my mother; and she was carrying a little navy blue box in her hands.

"Ah there you are, come here" she said.

I did as I was told and stood before her.

"Yes mum?" I said.
She then held the box towards me.

"Your Grandfather told me he had a lovely time last night, and asked me to give you this; he's sleeping at the moment" she explained.

Is that all he told her? Nothing about how we were attacked?
Is she even aware of what apparently happened to my father?
Does she even know or believe these so called creatures even existed?

I was tempted to ask, but thought it best not to in case she thought I was going insane; wouldn't blame her in the least though.

"What's this?" I asked.
"Well you have to open it to find out silly" she said playfully.

I then took the lid off and to see a black cross with a silver inner cross and red rubies at each point and a large one in the middle.

"Wow" I said.
I had to admit, it was beautiful.
"Don't forget to thank him when you see him" She said.

I simply nodded and smiled.

"Well, I'm off, not working today. So feel free to go out and what not like, I'll be looking after your great grandfather today" she smiled sweetly and brushed her hand down my cheek, then made her way to the kitchen.

I looked down at the cross again and ran my fingers over the rubies; I pulled it out the box and saw it had a black velvet rope for the chain.

I then put it around my neck and tied it. I returned back into the living room and went over to the large mirror above the fireplace.
Had to say, it looked good on me.

I slightly smiled and made my way back to my room.
For some reason I was feeling tired again, so I jumped back into bed and drifted.

Night: I found myself in a forest and for some reason, I was running and I couldn't stop.
I just kept going and going, rushing past hundreds of trees.

I turned behind me and to my horror I saw the same guy that came after me and my Grandfather. But he was rushing behind me with his eyes firing red and crimson blood dripping from his mouth.

"You're not getting away this time boy!" he screamed in a psychotic tone.

I turned back ahead of me and kept running, after what seemed like hours of running, I bumped harshly into something and fell onto my back.

I looked up and saw a man towering over me, light skin and blonde haired; however with the hat on his head, the darkness covered his eyes. He extended his hand to me and I reached out my hand, he pulled me up then I could feel his eyes on me; as if he was judging me by the way I looked. Next thing I knew he shoved me behind a tree.

"Stay there" he simply said.

His voice was calm but firm, not complaining of course I did as I was told. I poked my head around the corner and saw that guy who was chasing me, standing in front of the person who saved me.

Suddenly in a flash of red and a painful anguish filled scream the creature fell on his knees and fell into a permanent sleep.

"Come here" said the man that saved me.

I did as I was told, slowly but carefully moving close to him.
He then reached out towards my neck I slightly jolted back pushing my back against the tree.

I then felt something slightly lifted from off my chest. I looked down and saw it was the Cross pendant that I put on.

"This should help you in the future" he said.
I wasn't sure what to say so I remained silent.
"I would know I have one" he continued.

He then reached down to his neck and pulled out a small kind of lace, then at the end of it was the exact same cross that I was wearing.
However, before I could ask him where he got it from…
I woke up.

I shot up from lying down, breathing in and out heavily.
"Whoa, what a dream" I gasped out

I then turned to my side table to see what the time was.
Immediately I fell out of bed because it was 7:45 pm!

"Oh crap!" I yelled.
I quickly rushed to the bathroom and had a shower in 5 minutes, 10 minutes to go.
Rushed to get dressed, slapping on black jeans and a white shirt.
"That'll do" I said.

With those five minutes left I grabbed my wallet and keys and ran out my room, down the stairs and out the front door.
Jumped into the car and sped off, luckily she only lives four minutes away.

7:15 now, I was late. Double checked myself then ran up to her door.
I knocked and took a breath and breathed out.
Seconds later the door opened and there was Jenifer.
Hands on her hips, not too pleased.
I smiled sheepishly.

"Hi Jen" I said.
"You're late" she said flatly.

"Sorry. I didn't feel well earlier so took a nap and overslept" I explained.
"Well you can make up for it by taking me to dinner"

With that she grabbed her bad and closed the door behind her then linked arms with mine.

Jennifer Saunders: my Girlfriend.
Red hair, green eyes and light skin. Sadly I have to say I'm losing my attraction towards this girl.
The "Spark" between us is not there anymore.
But still debating if we should part or not, truth is told she only stays with me because I'm rich.
So in the car we went and headed for town for our dinner.

<u>Chapter 9</u>

"Out with it lads" I said as I took a seat under the tree.
Zack sighed and rested his back against the tree as he sat on a branch.

"It wasn't long after we left the village that we got into the city, it was an average place; as in just enough humans around to kill a few and not get caught" he explained.
I nodded and kept looking up at him to tell him to carry on.

"We came to one of the parks, usually popular with young adults, but we saw a teen and an old man instead. Seemed like a good mix of blood together; so I thought it best to get them"
He then took a moment and breathed in while pushing his hair back.

"Keep going" I said like an anxious child.
"Alright, alright, I rushed around the surrounding area to distract them, and it worked. I finally stopped and hid in a tree quite close to them.
I leapt out and grabbed the kid by his shoulders, but the bastard punched me in my chest and I went flying backwards landing on my back.
But that wouldn't keep me down, I flipped back onto my feet and stood ready, I looked at the lad then went charging at him, but with a bit of excess speed I went to the bushes; gave them a bit of a scare" he spoke proudly as he stretched.

I rolled my eyes thinking he shouldn't be so proud since they apparently 'Got away', but if I stated that then I know he wouldn't tell me the rest.
So I smirked at him pretending I was impressed.

"I jumped out again and kicked him in the back and let him to kiss the ground, and then back into the bushes; got them pretty panicked. The lad quickly shot up trying to get himself and the old man out.
But I wasn't going to let that happen. I ran out and tightly gripped his shoulders and threw him on one of the park benches" he continued.
I slightly bit my lips and my eyes widened as I was more intrigued by the story.

"I then stood up over him, ready to deliver the final blow. Suddenly a flash of silver came flying out from the old man and the kid caught it. I suddenly felt strangely weak, I noticed he held the sign of God in his hands; so I fled" he said with slight shame in his voice.

"No one had ever defended against me, especially with a cursed cross, almost like the old man knew about us and what we do outside our village" he explained.

"Well, that's odd. Where were you Dylan?" I asked.

"I went hunting elsewhere but found Zack in time to watch him run" Dylan answered.

"Oh shut up!" Zack screamed "I'm going to bed, besides daylight will be here soon" with that he sped off to his home.

"Well I'm off too Ana, so should you" said Dylan.
He then left. I sighed and ran back home.

Once inside I quickly closed the door and ran around the house closing off any possibly gap where light could get in.
I then went to my room and got changed, I then lay down on my bed and closed my eyes.

As I lay there, I couldn't get Zack's story out my head, who were those humans got away.
The more I thought about it...the more curious I was.
Were they warriors? Slayers? Or just normal humans?
Despite my thoughts I felt myself drifting to sleep.

Chapter 10

A good few hours had passed now; Jen and I had finished our dinner and were now walking back to the car.

It was that time in winter when it would always get dark very quickly, and considered what happened the other evening I just wanted to drop her and speed home.

The town was rather busy so we had to park quite a distance from the restaurant unfortunately we had quite a walk ahead.

"You ok?" she asked me.

"Oh yeah, just great" I responded

"Let's cut through the park" she said as she linked arms then began to pull me towards it.

But once again memories of the other night washed over my mind.

"Jen-"I started.

"Oh come on Lee, it'll be romantic" she whined.

I rolled my eyes then nodded; she tightened her grip on my arm and rested her head on my shoulder as we proceeded forward.

"It's a nice night don't you think?" she tried to sweetly ask. I simply sighed and nodded.

"Something wrong Lee?" she questioned

"I...I just feel a bit off, sorry"

"But you've been like this since you've picked me up!" she exclaimed.

"So?! What if I have?! Can't you just drop it?!" I yelled at her as I pulled my arm free.

"That's it! I've had enough of your attitude, you don't treat me like you used to!" she screamed.

"That's because I'm sick of you!" I screamed back.

On that note she ran away from me, I sighed In realisation of how I just spoke to her.

"Oh Christ almighty" I groaned

It then came to my attention how unsafe of area we were in, I may not love her anymore; but I didn't want her hurt, so I proceeded in the direction she ran in.

"Jen! Jennifer where are you?!" I yelled hoping she would hear me.

Sadly no answer, so I carried on walking; maybe she was so upset she didn't answer and was hiding somewhere.
Suddenly I heard laughing.

"Who's there?!"
"Awe, I think he's lost someone" I heard a voice say.
"It's sad really, but then again after that fight, it would seem he doesn't really care that much" said another.
"Show yourself you cowards!" I screamed as I spun around looking in all directions.

"If you insist" they said in unison.
I then turned behind me and saw two teenage boys, both twins and around 17 years old.

"Where is she?" I demanded.
"Who?" one said.

They both had black raven hair and green eyes with pale skin. But one was wearing a dark red top and the other a sandy brown top.

"Jennifer, where is she?" I asked again
"Oh does she have red hair and green eyes?" asked the one in red.
"And pal skin about 5ft 4?" added the other.
"Yes, she is" I answered.

As I spoke I had reached my hand up my neck and felt for necklace.
"Nope, haven't seen her" they both laughed.
I found the pendant and pulled it out showing it to them.
"Tell me or you'll regret it!" I said firmly.
"Ok, ok!" they said.

Then they boy in the sandy brown top jumped up into the tree.
"Where is he going?" I asked.
"He'll be back" said the remaining twin.

Suddenly then I heard crunching and snapping of branches and out from the tree fell a body.

"Oops, my mistake!" yelled the other twin who jumped down landing on the branch.
"Was that her?" they asked.

I gasped and ran over to the body; I pulled her so she lay on her back.
"J...Jen?" I stuttered.

I screamed in anguish as I held my cross up to them, but before I could
weaken them...they had gone.

"Just so you know, her blood was divine" I heard them say, followed by a
long painful silence. They had gone now.

I looked down at her and carefully pulled her into the light.
Her skin had turned pasty and cold; I saw she had a deep gash splitting
into her neck with blood still leaking out.
The sight of her body brought tears to my eyes she didn't deserve this.
And because of me a person I loved has lost their life.

Memories of our time together came into my mind and how much time we
good times we had. Then it occurred to me, what was I to do now?

If I told her parents what happened I know they would call me crazy.
So I had to lie, just tell them we got attacked, I bent down to the floor
and smeared mud over my top and face.
I then tore parts of my shirts; at least now I look like I was in a fight.

Finally I reached down to Jennifer's neck and gathered some blood on my
fingers and spread some on my chest, arms, fists and face.
I then reached for my phone and sat by her side.
"I'm so sorry" I whispered.
I then called for an ambulance.

Chapter 11

My eyes fluttered open from my sleep.
I yawned and stretched my arms as I lay there feeling too lazy to get out of bed.

Suddenly then my door swung open and Krish came in.
"Evening sister, wake up" he said cheerfully.
"What the hell are you so happy about?" I groaned.
"Sit up properly and I'll tell you" he said.

I sighed and sat up crossing my legs; Krish then sat on my bed and turned to face me.

"I overheard Odion and Max talking to father about having their first hunt outside the Village" he explained.

"What?! That's unfair! They're only 17, how could he allow them to go out?!" I moaned.

"Because they're old enough" he said
"Earth to Krish! I'm 18 and I have been for 200 years! He doesn't let me out!" I screamed.
"Because you're a girl, and father doesn't want you hurt" he explained.

I sighed and rested against my bed head folding my arms in annoyance.
"This is unfair!" I whined.

"Well ask him; besides I know you can take care of yourself, but you know what he's like" he explained.
I sighed in annoyance as I did indeed know what father would say.

"Well come on, have to see Odion and Max off soon" he added.
With that he stood up and walked out.

Still annoyed I pulled myself out of bed and got dressed. As I was brushing my hair I pulled back my thick curtains and let the moonlight fill my room.

I then proceeded out the door tossing my brush on the bed as I did so.
"Hello Anastasia" said a kiddie voice.

I looked down and saw Mina, my youngest sibling.
As adorable as a kitten and deadly as poison, that's how I would sum her up; but she's nice to me which is fine. Just not to Odion, Max or Ray and Laura.

This again is fine with me.
"Hi Mina, you ok?" I asked.
"I'm fine" she sweetly said smiling.

"Good what are you up to?" I said.
"Nothing, I'm bored; play a game with me?" she asked.
"I can't I'm going to see father first, I'll play later, go ask Charlotte or Anaie" I told her.
"Oh...Ok" she said. Clearly not happy but still walked away.

I simply rolled my eyes and lightly laughed.
I carried on going through the house until I got outside, I sighed as I sat on the steps.

"Guess what we're doing this evening" I head two voices say.
I groaned as I turned around to see Odion and Max standing either side of me smirking.

"Go away you morons!" I said as I turned back around.
"I knew she'd be jealous" said Odion who was wearing his favourite red shirt.
"Then we've done our bits for this evening to piss off our big sister" added Max.
"I hate you two" I said.
"We know" they responded.

They both walked past me ruffling my hair.
I groaned in annoyance as I pushed my hair back.
After being on my own for a while I heard a voice calling me into the house, so I pushed myself off the stair and into the house; as soon as I walked through the door Father was standing there.
Darien Scarlet King. My father and leader of the Red Rose Clan.
He was one of the powerful and fairly respected men in the village.

I had even heard that one day, after hearing strange noises outside during the day, he had ran out and swiftly killed the group of men that were walking about and managed to get inside before the sun melted his skin clean off his bones.
Then come nightfall everyone saw slaughtered bodies drowned in their own blood outside the village hall.
I was even told that hundreds of years ago when Vampire Hunting was more common with Hunters, Father had fought off 30 humans that were surrounding out Village.
He suffered multiple injuries but still survived and healed after two days.

"There you are Anastasia, how are you?" he asked.
"Very well thank you father" I answered.
"Good, now come along, we must proceed to the Village Hall; all of us will wish Odion and Max good luck on their first evening out of the forest" he spoke proudly.

I rolled my eyes and sighed.
"Yes Father, but can I not set foot out of the Village?" I asked sternly.
"Ana, we've been through this, your skills are more suited to protect the village, not to go out hunting" he explained.

"In other words, you don't want me to leave" I said blankly.
"No…yes, Ana please; you're my eldest daughter and as one of the younger- yet stronger generation I do not want you hurt, besides you are unable to perform such tasks. You do not have the skill for it." he responded.

"But father if humans do come in and armed and I do get hurt it would be too late anyway, I do have the skill can I not prove it to you?" I cheekily said.

"Ana please! You are not allowed on the human's side, you will remain here!" he shouted at me.

I was not even going to try and retaliate, so I just left it at that, I just stormed out and made my way to the Village Hall.

Once inside I sat on one of the twenty benches inside and waiting for anyone else to come in.
Not long after waiting, near enough everyone in the Village came in and sat down facing the front. I however sat far in the back row.
Then in came father, followed by Odion and Max with mother behind them.

"Good evening everyone, we would like to thank you all for coming today so we can wish my sons good luck" he said proudly.

Everyone then clapped and cheered everyone but me. Just then I felt someone sit next to me, I turned and saw it was my brother Krish.

"Hi" he simply said.
"Hello, shouldn't' you be at the front?" I asked
"I could say the same thing to you" he responded.
"Well I'm not going to because I don't want to" I said as I folded my arms.

"How about tomorrow we ask father if you and me go out, I know he won't let you go alone; but us together would be better anyway" he explained.

I have to admit he did have a good point; and we do work well together. "Well I supposed we could ask him, but I did ask him earlier and well…" I continued.

"You asked him on your own and he gave you a poor excuse which was another way of saying no; and then actually said no" he said

"Um…how did you know that?" I asked.
"Oh, I was in the room next door when he said it" he cheekily answered. I narrowed my eyes and glared at him.

"Congratulation my sons, I'm very pleased to send you to the human side for your first hunt, and as usual; I want some of the blood of your first kill to be stored in this vile" said my father.

He then handed them a single glass vile with a cork pushed in the top. "Of course father" both Odion and Max replied.

"Excellent; now off you go boys" father exclaimed as he embraced them both.
"Be careful my darlings" said my mother as she two embraced her twin boys, followed with a round of applause and cheers from the rest of the villagers.

Odion and Max exited the hall and proceeded into the forest.
Despite how annoyed I was I still wished my little brothers good luck.

<u>**Chapter 12**</u>

An ambulance had arrived and taken her inside; I went in and sat by her side holding her hand.

Tears slid down my face as I looked upon her bloody body, I dearly hoped nothing would have happened this evening; but how wrong I was.

I closed my eyes praying that there was some ray of hope that she would survive, but the only thing that was running through my mind were those two monsters.

They looked so young but still had no mercy on her.
Not long into my thoughts did we finally arrive at the hospital; Drs and Nurses rushed her into the emergency room.
I however had to remain outside; I rested my hands in my head and closed my eyes.

"God please save her; I beg you" I lightly sobbed.

Time had passed a great deal and I still remained in my seat praying for her survival.
I suddenly felt a hand on my shoulder; I got slightly up to meet with one of the Doctors.

"Mr V.Hsing?" he asked as he looked down at me.
"Yes Doctor" I said as I stood up with my hands pressed together with hope.
"I'm sorry Sir, she had a severe lack of blood; and sadly we were unable to restore it" he explained.

I fell back in the seat in horror, in disbelief and sorrow.

"No…" I whispered.
"I am so very sorry, we've already contacted her parents, and they're on their way here" he said as he placed a reassuring hand on my shoulder.

I then suddenly heard doors slam open and in came running Jennifer's mother and father. Her mother Hannah ran to the Doctor and gripped onto his right arm while her red eyes poured out more tears.

"Where's my daughter?!" she screamed.

The Doctor motioned his hand to the room in front of us and she forced the doors open still crying.
Then in came John who walked over to me.

"Hi Lee, what happened Son?" he asked.

I froze for a moment before answering, didn't want him thinking I was crazy.

"We…were, attacked; by monsters" I stuttered to say.
"Nowhere is safe nowadays, don't worry lad; but by the look of you it was quite a struggle, thank you for trying to fight for her life" he said as he rested a hand on my shoulder.
Except for I didn't do a thing to help, if anything I feel at fault for ever saying 'yes' to going through that park and for shouting at her.

"Thank you Sir" I said.
"Go home lad, we'll take it from here" said John.

I went outside the building and saw the usual line of taxis around the side; I got in one then told the man to take me back to the city.

Once there I slowly made my way back to my car.
I rested back in my chair thinking and hoping my mother wouldn't see me when I walked in.

Chapter 13

Hours had passed since Odion and Max had left, and everyone was going about their nightly business.

Children playing, women gossiping and men sitting around, telling stories of events that happened to them in the past.

I however was wondering around the outside of the village in the forest. After a while of walking I soon came to the lake, certainly one of the most beautiful parts of the forest.

Especially since the sky was clear this evening the stars were glistening and the moon was full; so the lake looked as beautiful as the night sky above.

I sighed as the fresh smell of the water lilies floated in the air.

I made my way over to the tree stump that I usually sit on, and closed my eyes. Then thoughts of the outside world began to cross my mind. Have to say that I was very curious to know how they have evolved, what have the invented and developed over all these years.

However anyone who visits the outside was forbidden to talk about what they saw, in order to prevent anyone from wanting to leave.

It was unfair because I have been dying to ask Zack and Dylan what the outside world was like, and how those humans now live life since we haven't had any come around here for many years.

Suddenly I heard laughing and the sound of two people walking, I remained still and opened my eyes.

I then slightly sniffed the air and relaxed myself again; it was only Odion and Max.

"So, how was the hunt boys?" I asked quite loudly.

"It was pretty amazing Ana, such a shame you couldn't see the outside world; it's very different" said Odion.

"Yes such a shame Ana, we even had out first kill, a weak little red haired girl; she was crying and terribly upset so…we put her out of her misery" carried on Max.

They both came into view from the bushes; I saw that Max was holding the vile that father gave them, filled with crimson red blood.

"And here's our proof" they both said as Max held up the vile.

On that note they left laughing back to the village, they already gloated enough to me so I saw no reason to return to the village just yet.

Chapter 14

Morning had finally come, last night felt like a bad dream
That was until I looked on the floor to see my white shirt that was covered in her blood.
I sighed as I sat up in bed and rested my head in my hands.

"Mum's bound to find out soon about what happened to Jennifer, but...I'll have to lie to her like I did with Jen's parents"

I suddenly heard a knock at the door and rapidly reached for my shirt and threw it under the bed and jumped back into bed.
Then in came my mother.

"Morning lazy bones" she said as she walked across my room and pulled the curtains.

The flash of light hurt my eyes so I pulled my covers back over my head.

"Oh come on!" she groaned at me as I felt her hit my head.

I slowly popped my head out and sat up in bed again, I rested my back against the headboard for a while before getting out of bed and getting dressed.

Once ready I made my way downstairs and into the kitchen, and was very worried at what I saw once there.
Sitting at the worktop table was my mother, Grandfather and the Police.
My eyes widened and my heart stopped.

"Lee...takes a seat please" stuttered my mother as a slight tear dripped down her face.

What was I going to do now? How would I explain what the hell happened last night?
I nodded and sat down next to my mother.

"Now, Mr V.Hsing" started the policeman
A serious stern expression on his face didn't make me feel any better about the matter.

"We're here to ask you questions involving your deceased girlfriend Miss Jenifer" he explained.

"Yes Sir" I said as I looked at him, then glancing at my mother every now and then.

"We understand that you both went out to dinner last night and by the end of the evening she was killed at the local park" he continued.

"That's right" I answered.
"How did this happen?" he asked me

"Well we felt it would be nice to stroll through the park, however I have to say that as of late I haven't been feeling like myself, I could see that Jennifer picked up on that. She then asked me what was wrong, I said nothing but she kept persevering for an answer from me" I explained.

"However I still didn't want to answer her, so out of nowhere I told her to leave me alone in a harsh tone" I lied, and I had to keep lying unless I wanted to be called crazy and accused of being the killer.

"Go on" said the Policeman.
"She then ran off, I felt terrible about what I said so I went after her" I continued.

I then took a deep breath and sighed.
"But by the time I found her, she had been killed. I proceeded to her body to check for any hope of life, but only a few steps from her was I tackled by another person. But his face was covered so I didn't see who it was" I proceeded to explain.

"He was armed with a knife and despite a bit of a struggled with him he finally ran odd, hoping the coast was clear I ran over to Jen and beheld her bleeding body; I touched her face and felt her pulse; sadly nothing happened, no sign of life. So I rang an ambulance. They came not long after and we were both taken to the hospital" I explained.

"It seems she was slashed in the back with what is guessed a knife and suffered severe bloody loss as well as a broken arm and spine" he explained.

I then remembered that the injuries could have been from when those creatures dropped her corpse out of the tree.

"That...that's horrible" I said slightly surprised.
"We know that despite you being her boyfriend, you are still under suspicion; unless you had any reason to want to hurt her" he firmly said as he looked me dead in the eye as if I really was her killer.

But my eyes were still, it was my fault she died but; I did not kill her.

"I had nothing against my girlfriend, I loved her too much to do anything to her" I responded calmly.

He however said nothing and wondered a few steps away.

"I see, well thank you for your time. Have a nice day" he politely said as he made his way out the door, followed by my mother to show him out; leaving me with my Grandfather.

"Do you now understand the magnitude of the situation Gabriel?" he asked me

I rested my head in my hands and sighed.

"But how, how is something like this possible?" I asked "Surely attacks like this do happen, why aren't they reported, why is nothing done?" I questioned my grandfather.

"My boy do you honestly expect normal people to believe that such creatures are roaming our planet? No, such people are too logical to be able to understand the complex history of the darker side of life, for you see lad; this has been happening for centuries" he explained.

I looked up at him keen and wanting to learn more.

"Come with me" he said.

I slowly stood up and followed him; I then saw he was leading me to the library.

Once there he closed the door and motioned for me to sit down. So I did. He then walked once again to the bookshelf in the far right of the room and pulled out the same red book he did before.

He placed it in front of me and opened the first page, and on there I saw a detailed black and white drawing of the same cross that I received; and titled next to it was VHS Hunter Clan.

"My boy, you have descended from a long line of vampire hunters" he said.
"Vampire Hunters?" I repeated, still slightly unsure.

"Yes Gabriel, Vampire hunters. I myself am one too, but because of your fathers valiant help I was able to live" he explained slightly chocking on his words.

"You see my boy, this battle between humans, vampires and vampire hunters has been going on for a very long time. The first occurrence of these events was in Romania. A very popular place for these dark creatures that in fact nearly the entire land was inhabited by them" he took a deep breath, and slowly breathed out; then turned to the next page.

"Jedediah was the creator of the Vampire Hunter clan that our family descended from, it was said that he saw his own mother and father slaughtered before his very eyes, and from then began expanding the clan with numbers of friends and family and have been killing Vampires since" he continued.

"Gabriel, are you aware of the meaning behind your surname?" he asked me?
"VH.Sing?" I said "No...what does it mean?" I asked.
"My boy, it stands for Van Helsing" he said

I froze for a minutes and my mind wondered.

"The same name I've seen in movies and books?"
"Gabriel, it's not a name of fantasy, it is truly real and you along with me are the last of the clan. As time went on since the birth of the clan we separated all around the world, and there are very few friends and family left" he explained.

"Why is that?" I asked
"As time passed the tradition of protecting humans was let go as there was not many Vampires around, so the number of hunters dropped" he answered

"I see" I said.
"However, time caught up with us. The number of Vampires has become greater than the number of hunters" he continued.

Have to say that all this history has greatly surprised me, I didn't know anything about my family history, and now I've been told I descend from a long line of Vampire Hunters.

"So here we are today, low number, back to bloodlust and a war with these creatures of darkness" he finally said.

I rested back and sighed as I ran my left hand firmly through my hair.
"So, you now know about our family history Lee" said a voice.

I stood up and spun around to see my mother standing in the door way, her arms wrapped around herself with tears dripping down her face from her weak red eyes.
"Mum?" I said

She just smiled at me as she walked in closing the door behind her.

Chapter 15

Despite being so far away from the Village I could still hear shouts of cheers and congratulations from everyone.

They were celebrating Max and Odion's victory. Big deal, I killed a human at the age of eight but you don't see them throwing a parade for me.

I sighed as I looked into the sky.

"Life is so depressing here" I said to myself
There was still a few hours left before sunrise so I thought I would go back to the village and talk to Mariana.

So I began to make my way back to the village, I saw Mina running around with several other kids playing games.

"Hi Anastasia!" she playfully yelled as she ran past me.
"Hello Mina" I responded as I walked past them all continuing my way to Mariana's small cottage.

It was the usual atmosphere in the village, playful peaceful and calm; how boring.
I made my way to Mariana's house, honestly for a woman that was 400 years old she actually didn't look that old, other than the fact Vampires don't age, none the less; it looked as if she was turned into a Vampire between her late thirties and early forties.
I gently knocked on the door and awaited an answer.

"Come in Anastasia" I heard Mariana said.

I did as I was told and sat on the floor opposite her near the fire.

"Now what can I do for you Anastasia?" she asked softly.
"I was hoping you would tell me a few stories Mariana, about the past" I responded as I made myself more comfortable.

"Very well" she said as she rested back in her chair.
"The one about the final battle years ago in Romania" I said like a child wanting to hear a bedtime story.

She deeply sighed and pulled her black blanket higher up her body.

"It was many years ago in Romania our supreme race was at war with all humans and Vampire Hunters alike"

I may have been a struggle to survive then, but I assure you, every day was an adventure. Prey was easier to come across, and more humans feared us more them than now" she started

"Sounds as if that was the prime of our Race Mariana" I commented.
"Indeed it was child, life was more exciting and in that part of the world, sunlight rarely reached us. We were able to roam freely in the day as we could at night. Indeed a more beautiful time for us" she continued.

"Tell me Mariana, why was there a war?" I asked

"One of the most shocking events in history, the attempted union of human and Vampires"

"Union?" I asked
"A human and a vampire wanted to wed" she carried on.

I leaned forward wanting to hear more.

"A disgusting union, thank goodness it did not take place. Such a thing should never happen; humans are food to us not an aspect of love" she continued.

"Certainly seems un-natural"
"Oh it certainly is child, even up to this day your father calls it a 'sin' " she explained.

Honestly I'm not surprised, father being as proud as he is, it certainly sounded like something he would say; not that he had much of a choice. I then stood up and walked to the window, the sky appeared lighter than earlier; dawn was coming.

"Morning is nearly here Mariana, I should take my leave" I said as I made my way to the door.

"Very well child, I shall see you then next night, then if you wish I could tell you the rest of the story" she said.

I nodded and smiled at her.

"Yes, thank you Mariana"

With that I left her cottage and preceded home everyone was preparing to settle in for the day; gathering the children and clothes and so on.

Soon I arrived at my home and on the steps was my little sister Anaie.
She sat there gazing into the starry sky, I'm not even sure if she knew I
was there or not.

"Anaie?" I said
She slightly moved her head down to look at me.
"Hello Anastasia" she said dully.

I have to say out of the whole village she was the most reserved person.
Always keeping to herself; never talking to anyone and always alone. It
was almost rather scary really.
She was somewhat different to the family and it yet escapes us as to
why... she had from what I last saw blonde hair and green eyes.

"How are you?" I asked
"Fine" she sighed.

Reserved and slightly bad mannered, but she was a younger sibling so I
decide to show a bit more caring than being just as ill-mannered back.

"You best be going inside Anaie, dawn is coming" I said.

She merely nodded and stood up and dragged herself into the house.
I rolled my eyes and shook my head at her.

"Children" I said flatly as I too made my way inside.
"Evening dear sister" I heard a voice say from the east corridor.
I turned and saw Krish.

"Hello Krish" I said as I proceeded to sit before the fire.
"Something the matter?" he asked as he walked towards the fire and sat
beside me.

"Well no nothing is wrong, but I did speak to elder Mariana" I explained.
"I see, what you spoke about?" he asked

Before answering him I glanced out the window and saw more brightness
take over the sky, I quickly stood up and closed the shutters blocked out
the light; as I was doing so Krish helped me with the rest of them.
Soon the room was full of darkness and the only light was of that of the
warm fire.

"You were saying" he said to me as he sat back down before the fire.
"Well I asked her to tell me a story about life from hundreds of years ago"
I started.
"Really, what story did she tell you?" he said

I then sat down next to him and sighed.

"About life in Romania, how our species could roam around in the day for it was as dark as night; how our feed was always on supply and how much greater our numbers were then than now" I explained in a slightly dreamy voice.

Indeed life did sound blissful- at least compared to the present time it did...sort of.

"Shouldn't you both be sleeping?" we heard a voice say.

Turning around we saw it was our mother Ariana, a typical Goddess. Lush black hair and stunning blue eyes and all topped off with her beautiful tanned skin.

"Yes mother, but Anastasia was just telling me a little story" explained Krish.

"What about?" she asked as she knelt down to us.
"Life in Romania all those years ago" I said.

"Ah, indeed a prosperous time for our race my children; it was truly a glorious time for us, however as you can see it was not meant to last" she said.
 "Anyway, off to bed you two" she continued.

We nodded and pushed ourselves off the floor and separated into our rooms.

Chapter 16

"You know about all this?" I asked

"Of course dear, you didn't think being married to your father for so many years and knowing him since he was 17, that I wouldn't know about him and his origin did you?" she asked

I wasn't sure what to think or say. Once again I've been bombarded with information that devastated my soul. I adjusted myself on the sofa and deeply sighed.

"You know it was a long time ago in secondary school when your father and I met" she started.

"It was quite strange really how we first met, I was in year 9 and he was in year 10; I also had a little brother, Connor" she took a breath.

"It happened in early March, Connor and I had to walk home, we decided to go through the fields at the back of the house to get home; however the only thing I can remember was being thrown across the field into a tree; and I passed out" she explained.

As she spoke I could hear tremors in her voice.

"When I regained consciousness, I looked around; but I could not see my little brother anywhere. So I ran home, only then I realised it was about 6pm and school ended three hours ago" she continued.

"When I got home I explained to my parents that I lost Connor, as well as what happened in the field. Mother comforted me for hours while father was on the phone to the police.
I eventually fell asleep crying and come morning, I didn't go to school; not eating, drinking or even getting out of bed. The shock of losing my younger brother devastated me. But not as much as to what was going to happen the next evening" she said.

Her eyes filled with tears as she stood before the fire wrapping her arms around herself.

"Mother and Father had gone to the police station to forward the investigation on Connor, they left me with a babysitter" she continued.

"I had my bath and she had given me my dinner and at 8pm we sat down to watch television. There was then a knock at the door, she told me she would be right back and to wait there.
It was seconds later did I hear a painful scream; I ran from the living

room to the door; there laying in the doorway was the babysitter screeching in agony and holding onto her neck which was gushing out blood" she paused for a moment, then cleared her tears from her eyes.

"I ran to the phone and dialled 999 but just as there was an answer the phone was knocked out of my hand, I turned to a small shadowed figure who was breathing heavily" she carried on as she place her hand over her heart.

"I didn't know what to do, so I ran to my room; but as I did I could hear footsteps running rapidly behind me along with the horrific screams of the babysitter downstairs begging for her life to be spared" I could now see tears dripping from her face onto the floor and she began stuttering with her words.

"I slammed my door closed and pushed my chair against the door handle. A sudden t...thudding nearly knocked the chair out of place; I covered my m...mouth trying not t...to scream. But it wasn't any good. The door suddenly broke in and the figure stepped inside my room and the light revealed to me the most shocking sight of my life. My little brother Connor" she blurted out in pain and sorrow as her became breathing unsteady.

Grandpa walked over to her and helped her to sit on the sofa; I rested a hand on her back trying to comfort her.

"It's ok dear" Grandpa said reassuringly.
"I'm fine" she said.

"I gasped as I stepped towards him softly speaking his name. But I looked into his eyes, I jumped back far from him; they were as red as blood. He took a step towards me and spoke in a raspy voice 'What's wrong sister? Not happy to see me?' he said" she lightly breathed in.

"I was so scared I backed further away. 'Come on, give your brother a hug' he spoke, but as he smiled; so my horror I saw sharp fangs staring at me" she gulped.

"I stepped towards him but instead of hugging him, I shoved him aside and ran down the stairs and out the back door to the fields. I hid behind a tree and rested trying to get my breath back. I then suddenly heard a voice, 'we're a bit too old to be playing games' I screamed and jumped back as I looked up to see Connor in the tree.
'It's your fault you know' he said to me as he jumped down 'It's your fault I'm this way now' "she continued.

"My eyes filled with tears at his words, 'Alison help me, please. I'm going insane, I'm craving blood. I just killed that girl…and…and now I want you!' he screamed as he lunged himself at me" she gasped.

"I jumped back and he remained still. 'I'm sorry' he softly spoke. 'I can't help it, I'm craving blood, my skin is as cold as death and my heart, Alison I can't feel my heart, it's stopped' he cried".

My own heart was breaking at this story; I even felt tears fill my own eyes.

"I ran to hug my poor little brother but was harshly pushed out the way onto the floor, I looked up and saw a tall figure with blonde hair and clothed in black. Gabriel Van Helsing, your father" she proudly said. "Stay away from him or you too will fall victim to becoming like these Demons" he said to me.

"I protested against his words saying that my brother would never harm me. He then turned to face me with piercing blue eyes and smirked at me…'I beg to differ' he said" she continued.

"He then pulled out a dagger from his pocket and made a small cut on his hand and shook it for a moment. I then looked at my brother who was gripping onto his hair screaming 'Stop it! The smell! I…I can't take it!' he wailed" she continued.

"He then lunged at your father and chased him across the field, leaving me alone. I turned and could faintly see two figures fighting on the field, I rushed over to them and as I did I saw your father pin Connor down by his clothes with a dagger. But before stabbing him with a wooden steak, I shoved him out the way and picked up the steak pointing it at him, telling him to stay away from my brother" she wrapped her arms tightly around herself.

" 'Look out!' he screamed at me, but too late I was tackled to the floor and I looked up to see my brother over me, hunger clear in his eyes" she said as more tears poured out of her eyes.

"I begged him to stop, but it seemed my pleas were doing nothing for me 'Alison, your blood smells so good!' he screamed as he leaned down and harshly bit into my arm. I felt very weak as I felt my blood being drained from my veins, he was then suddenly knocked off me, and I saw he had a dagger piercing in his shoulder. 'Look what you've done, drawn blood from your own sister!' your father screamed at my brother" she sighed and lightly breathed in.

"My brother sat up from the floor gasping in pain, he pulled the dagger out and threw it into the ground. He moved slightly back and there were light streams of blood trickling down the side of his mouth" she continued as her eyes once again filled with tears.

"He looked at his hands, then me, then your father. He tightly gripped his hair and began screaming at us 'Please, please kill me! Before I kill someone!' your father then pulled out a black gun from his belt and pointed it at Connor, 'I'm sorry sister, I love you; but never tell mother and father' he cried to me" she wept as she whipped the tears from her face.

"Your father steadied his gun, 'Forgive me Miss Alison' he said. I quickly spun around and as I did I heard the sound of a gunshot. My heart jumped and tears flooded my eyes. I slowly turned around to see my brother lifeless on the floor; I ran over and held his icy body in my arms. Even till today I feel responsible for my brother's death. But no one found out what was the cause of his death' despite the body being found" she then stood up and made her way to the door.

"Your father was merciful, and apologised to me again after that; then after the next day I went back to school. I met him in the school lunch room, we never talk about what happened that night since...anyway, well I'm off to bed my dear, see you in the morning" she then left the room in silence.

"You should rest too my Lad" my Grandfather said.

I nodded and made my way back to my room. I saw night had fallen fast and sadly I lost my appetite.
So I lay in bed letting my mother's heart wrenching story run through my mind; until I fell asleep.

<u>**Chapter 17**</u>

The morning and afternoon passed by quite quickly and glorious night fell. Once again our village was alive with our people walking around the streets and paths. I opened my window and could hear the children playing outside together.

After I got changed I went and sat in the living room. Not long after thinking to myself did I hear someone walk in. I turned around and saw my father Darien.

"Evening Anastasia" he said with a smile.
"Good evening Father" I responded.

He then proceeded forward and sat next to me.

"And how is my beautiful daughter today?" he asked.

I smiled and lightly laughed; hope he didn't think I forgot about what he said about me not being able to leave the Village to go on a hunt.

"I'm fine Father thank you" I answered.
"Anastasia, I hope you're not still upset about the other night" he started.
"No father" I responded.

Of course I'm still upset, what sort of question is that?

"Well, Krish spoke to me a few moments ago; regarding going outside to hunt. And well, he has managed to talk me into letting you go" he continued.

I think excitement was building inside me after hearing that.

"Providing you go with Krish" he swiftly added.

Then the excitement dropped once more. Not that I mind being with my dear brother, it's just it seemed that despite letting me out, it would only be if someone came with me.

I'm sure I'm not that weak, and I'll prove that I am not!

"Really father, that's wonderful. Thank you so very much" I said fairly cheerfully.

I then moved over and hugged my father tightly, and I felt him return my embrace.

"You're welcome my darling, but not tonight; tomorrow evening you may leave" he explained.

I wasn't going to be greedy so I took what I was offered instead of begging for more.

"Just promise me that you will be careful" he added.
I just nodded and smiled at him.

"Of course father, I promise" I sweetly said as I smiled again.
"Where's Krish father?" I asked as I stood up ready to run to where my brother was.

"I think he's in the village centre" he answered.

With my swift speed I rushed to the centre and within seconds I saw him and the speed I was going at caused him to fall back on the floor.

"Thank you! Thank you so much!" I exclaimed as I tightened my grip around him.

"Why don't I get hugs like that?" said a voice.

I turned to look around and saw Krish had been talking to Ray, Zack, Dylan and Ryan.

It then occurred to me that Ray asked that question.
"Because you don't deserve it!" I said.
"What are you thanking him for Ana?" asked Dylan.

"Thanks to my darling brother, I finally get my chance to go on my own hunt" I proudly said as I stood up.

"What?!" screamed two voices.

I smirked to myself and turned around to see Max and Odion, clearly not pleased at all.

"That is not right; I thought she wasn't allowed to set foot outside the village!" Max whined.

"Well she isn't" said a voice.
We all turned around and saw little Ryan standing there.

"Oh really?" said Odion.
"She can go...but with Krish" he explained as he turned and began to walk away.

"How did you know?" I asked him.
"I overheard from my room" he answered as he continued walking on.

"Awe, father wouldn't let you go without help I see" mocked Max.
"I don't mind, but at least I can go out at all" I sternly responded.

"Just be careful Ana" I heard Ray say.
"Goodness sake, why is everyone so worried? I am fully able to take care of myself" I groaned in annoyance.

I then helped Krish up from the floor.

"So, any idea on what kind of victim you're going to pick?" asked Zack.
"Well, not really. But now that you mention it, I'd like to pick out a man" I answered as I began to let my mind wonder.

It was indeed an interesting question, considering normally I would just kill anyone who walked into the village; I didn't put much thought into actually picking someone.

"Anyway, I'm going to enjoy this evening; that way tomorrow will come faster and Krish and I can go on our hunt. Enjoy your evening boys" I sweetly spoke as I proceeded past the boys.

I then decided I would go to the lake this evening, so I began to make my way there.
It was another glorious evening, the stars were gleaming brightly and the moon was beginning its transformation.
There was a light breeze blowing and I could smell the earth and fresh pine swirling in the air, I breathed in the sweet scent and sighed.

"This time tomorrow I'll be outside exploring the humans' world" I said to myself.

Soon I arrived at the lake, this time I sat near the edge of the lake and admired the view before me.

"You know Ana, it's not that great on the other side" I heard a voice say.
I spun rapidly around and saw Zack standing behind me with his arms folded.

"Good evening Zack. Why, what's wrong with their world?" I asked.

"They, well the humans appear much more intelligent that all those years ago. They're intelligence is amazing, when you go you will see what I mean, and in addition to that there are more chances of our lives being in danger. Not just by humans but by their creations" he explained

"Like, creatures?" I questioned.
"No Ana, it's more horrific than that. But you'll discover all that tomorrow evening" he said.

He then walked over and sat down beside me.

"Just be careful Ana. I don't want you to get hurt" he said, but he wasn't looking at me when he spoke.

"Zack please, I can manage myself thank you" I said in a light tone,
"I don't doubt you Ana, just be careful, that's all I ask of you" he repeated. I turned to face him and smiled.

"You amaze me Zack, your strength and your ruthlessness; sounds like me on a bad day" I lightly laughed.

After my comment I'm sure I saw him smile, and then turned his head to face me.

"I admire you also Anastasia, I admire how strong you are, not letting anything stand in your way; but you still respect your family and do as they ask" he softly spoke.

I never had the chance to speak to Zack properly, or even about the topic we were speaking now; it was quite pleasant.

"Thank you, but the truth is when all is said and done; family is all we have left in this world. So we should treasure them as the most precious things in our lives" I explained to him.

He simply nodded and turned to face the lake once more.

<u>**Chapter 18**</u>

Morning finally came leaving another painful evening behind.
I slowly opened my swollen eyes realising they were that way because of
my little cry before bed.

I sat up in bed and lightly pressed my fingertips on my eye lids.

"Christ, this is getting impossible, nearly every night for the past few days
I've gone to sleep with tears in my eyes" I said to myself.

"But what can me of all people do?" I asked.

Despite my endless wondering I finally attempted to get out of bed and
got ready for another stressful day filled with depression.

I made my way downstairs and proceeded to the kitchen, I poured myself
a glass of water and sat down at the table.
I sighed to myself and began to fiddle with my cross around my neck.

"There must be something, anything I can do. These creatures can't keep
going through life killing innocent people" I said.

Thoughts kept running through my mind as I let my mind think back on
everything that has happened over the last few days.

Every thought and memory filled me with anger, and I could still smell
fresh blood; which reminded me of Jennifer's gruesome death; her pale
face, slashed neck and bloodied body haunts my mind.

"Morning Gabriel" I heard a familiar voice say.

I spun around and saw it was my Grandfather, his eyes didn't exactly look
any better than mine; looks as if he also found it difficult to sleep.

"Morning Grandpa, how did you sleep?" I asked as I pulled back a chair
for him to sit on.

"Not very well Lad, your mother's story and past events brought tears to
my eyes most of the night" he explained as he sat next to me.

"Grandpa, is there...nothing that can be done about this?" I asked him
"You can't change the past my boy" he responded.

"No, I mean; can I do anything...to prevent this from carrying on?" I
asked again being more specific.

"Gabriel, I know only one solution but my boy; I can't allow you to put your young life at such risk" he said as he stood up and began wondering up and down the room.

"After all that has happened the least you can do is tell me" I pleaded.

"No, you will not suffer the same fate as your father, or else that will be the end of the Van Helsing Bloodline" he sounded more stressed now, so I decided not to ask any more questions on the subject.

"Ok Grandpa" I said, quickly I downed the rest of my water and went to the library.

I closed the door behind me and drew back the curtains letting in the glorious sunlight.
Looking around the room everything was glowing; I then turned my attention to the bookshelf that ran all along the far right wall.

"I know what I need to do, but only after I learn a bit more will it determine if I should do it and how I should do it" I said to myself.

I then walked to the far end of the bookshelf and found the red book Grandpa had shown me.

"If he won't tell me, I'll have to find out on my own"
I sat down on the long sofa and opened the book, there was still that picture of Great grandpa and dad together.
I smiled at the picture and placed it on the tea table, and then I turned to the first page; which had a small message written within a black border.

> ***"This book is for all members of the Van Helsing Clan.***
> ***Pass this down to each Generation so that in every life we can***
> ***continue to protect the human race as we have done for centuries;***
> ***and will continue to***
> ***Jedediah Van Helsing"***

I smiled proudly knowing I had descended from such a noble bloodline, I continued smiling as I turned to the next page and began reading in my head.

"The Van Helsing Clan began centuries ago in Romania on their noble and pure quest to rid the world of evil. Jedediah Van Helsing, the creator of the clan.
He made this decision because of the death of his parents.
It was said that his pregnant mother was taken into the local infirmary where she would give birth to his only sibling.

Sadly, just as Jedediah's parents arrived home; he saw his father being brutally murdered outside the house.

He rushed outside and the creature fled, he helped his mother who gave him the baby and ordered him to return to the house.

Reluctantly he did as he was told. Quickly he rested the baby on the bed surrounding it with pillows, and rushed outside to his parents; there he saw his mother had tried to help his father get back into the house.

Jedediah was going to rush out and help but his mother had told him to go back inside and close the door, and only open it if she knocked on it. Jedediah protested: with that creature still out there how could he leave his kin outside.

He took one more step towards them but was horrified when he saw a shadowed creature leapt out of the darkness, shoving both his parents to the ground.

His mother lost grip of his father and was forced to the floor and she screamed telling Jedediah to go back inside and protect his little sister.
He did as he was told and slammed the shack door behind him.
As he ran to the bedroom he could hear his mother's mournful cry of pain"

Tears fill my eyes up at the story; I couldn't imagine being in such a state it sounded too horrific.
"My God" I gasped.

"Once in the bedroom he saw his little sister sound asleep, he rushed over to her and lightly brushed a finger down her soft delicate cheek.
"I won't let anything happen to you, I promise on pain of death; I will not" he spoke to his sleeping sibling.

A suddenly crash of glass and the window fell in causing millions of glass chips scatter by the bedside.
In shock he lunged forward and stood before his little sister"

"This is horrific" I said to myself.

"In climbed a creature bathed in grey clothing; it stood before him; it's breathing rapid and shallow. Jedediah was in deep fear after seeing what was done to his parents; his only worry was what would happen to him and his little sister.
"Stand back you demonic creature!" he screamed.
"And let fresh young blood like yours go to waste? Not likely" it responded in a raspy voice.

As the candle light of the room shone on the creature I saw it was a man and with that evil on his face, I was even more horrified at the site of his teeth. Like an animals, so sharp and pointed, I stood my ground trying to protect my little sister"

I then stopped reading, and then I noticed that the point of view of the story had been changed.

"He wrote this himself" I whispered.
Wanting to know more, I carried on reading.

"The creature took one step towards me and licked its teeth, how I wish it would go away. I had committed no sins and my sister as pure as an angel would leave this world with me.

But a sudden screech filled scream and splash of red the creature fell to its knees before me and transformed into dust.
My hand over my pounding heart, and the other resting on the bed behind me.
I sat on the bedside and looked at my still sleeping sister, then before me again stood another figure.

"Who are you?" I asked as I stood back up again.
"Don't worry" he told me.
"I killed that Vampire that was going to kill you and your sibling" he said.

"Vampires...?" I asked at this point in my life; I had no idea what those creatures were.
'What are Vampires?' I asked him still keeping my guard up.

The man, or so he appeared to be wore black clothes and had a dark brown hat on his head, his skin appeared light and peachy, and his hair rested on his shoulders.
He walked towards my sister and looked down at her.

"Vampires are like children of the devil, their very existence is a sin" he said with hate.
"But, what else can you tell me?" I asked again.
"They appear in human form, but drink the blood of living humans" he explained.
"How horrible" I said, as I rested a hand around my neck.

The idea of demonic creatures stalking the planet by feasting on blood is horrifying."

Indeed it was and still is, horrified and heartbroken at the story, I read on.

"He looked down at my little sister once more and began to speak to me.
"I'm sorry in such a short time you've been orphaned" he said.

A light tear slid down my face at his hurtful, yet true words.

"It's alright, but without you my family line would end, so thank you" I
said with much gratitude.

"I understand the place of your parents is irreplaceable but, if you wish; I
would like to offer to look after you and your little sister" he said.
"W...would you?" I stuttered to ask.

He smiled at me.
"Of course, you're so young, as is your sister; and I can only imagine how
horrid it must be to be so alone in times like this"

I picked up my little sister and rocked her slowly in my arms.

"I don't even have a name for you dear sister" I sadly said to her.
"What was your mother called?" he asked me.
"Kathryn" I responded.
"You know lad, a mother is the most important person in your life, she
bared you for 9 months and gave you life; out of respect for her, give her
your mother's name" he explained.

He indeed made a good point, so I decided to do so, Kathryn"

I slowly closed the book and sighed. Jedediah must have written this
diary and I still have a lot to read.
But a great deal of time had passed and it was the late afternoon.

"Better eat something, then I'll read a bit more before bed" I said to
myself.

So I proceeded to the kitchen. As I walked through the house it looked as
if no one was home.

"Wonder if mum took Grandpa out"

As I walked around the kitchen deciding on what to eat, I then thought of
what Grandpa said earlier today.

About how I could help, I felt that after a bit more reading I would have
more than enough of a chance to try and take on those Vampires.

And why not, I'm sure my father would do the same thing, as would anyone in my bloodline.

I turned my attention back to food; so I heated up some soup and made my way back to the library.

Chapter 19

Zack stood up and began to walk away from me.

"I'm going back to the Village, take care Ana" he simply said.
"Oh, okay; goodbye Zack" I called back to him.

I was alone once again, as I sat there I couldn't help but think about what Zack and I were talking about; it was strange but interesting.

"Would be nice if we could get on like that more frequently" I said to myself as I pulled my knees to my chest and sighed.

Not long into my strange thoughts did I begin to feel a bit hungry.
With that I pushed myself off the floor and proceeded back to the village.
Once there I went in the food hut and deeply breathed in the smell of aged blood.

"Hmm, delicious; I think the ones near the back are the older ones, so they should have more flavour" I said as I lit a candle and closed the door behind me.

I slowly made my way down the hut to the far end, on the way I saw the shelves that were set from the bottom to the roof; stocked with bottles and jars filled with blood.

As I went further down I could see that the colour of the blood would darken depending on how long it's been there.
I reached the middle of the hut and picked up a clear jar holding scarlet red blood.

"That will do just fine" I said to myself.

Just as I was reaching for the jar the hut door opened, I froze before taking it and turning to see who it was.

In what little light there was I could see it was Ray. Rolling my eyes I took the jar and proceeded back out.

"Hello again Ana, how are you?" he asked me.
"Fine, until you asked Ray" I said as I passed him.
I heard him sigh just as I placed my hand on the door.

"Ana, I don't see why you behave in such a manner towards me, what have I ever done to you?" he frustratingly asked me.

"Ray Steinberg, you know all too well that I hate your obnoxious attitude"

I said as I pushed slightly on the door.

Suddenly I felt a hand on my shoulder; I spun around and met eyes with Ray.

"Ana, you also know despite that; I'm your parent's choice; anyway, you wouldn't want to disappoint them would you?" he slyly asked.

I reached my hand on top of his and dug my nail into his skin.

"That may be so, but I hope you're aware there are plenty more real men in this village" I responded as I let him go and left the hut.

Only after a minute or so of walking did I see Dylan and Zack.

"Evening Anastasia" Dylan said with a smile.
"Good evening" I said.
"Going somewhere, with that 35 year old blood?" Zack asked with a clear smirk on his face.

"As a matter of fact I was heading home; I was feeling hungry and a bit weak. This should help me; besides I'll need all the energy I can get for tomorrow" I said.

"Oh, that's right your first hunt" Dylan added.
"Yes, but you could have waited till you got home to eat" Zack said.

I was slightly confused at his words.
"I...haven't had any yet" I slowly said.

"Then why is there blood on your nails?" He asked.

I looked down at my hands and remembered I pierced Ray's hand earlier.

"Oh, I had a bit of a run in with Ray; never mind; anyway, I should be going; goodnight boys" I finished.
"Goodnight Ana" Zack said as he put a hand on my shoulder and began walking away.

"Sweet dreams Ana" Dylan said as he followed Zack back to their house.

I then carried on home; sunrise would be here soon; so I made my way to my room and closed my door.

As I sat on my bed I opened the jar and deeply breathed in the bloody smell.

"Hmm, divine" I said to myself, as I then started drinking the blood.

Not having too much did I start to feel very tired, I replaced the lid on the jar and got dressed in my lace night dress; then settled into bed yawning.

"Oh I look forward to tomorrow evening; it's been far too long since I got to shed the blood of a human".

I closed my eyes and let thoughts and memories fill my head as I eventually drifted off to sleep smiling.

<u>Chapter 20</u>

I had finished eating my food and took the red book with me back to my room.
I lay on my bed and flicked through to the last page I was on.

"I hope I learn a lot from this book, because I'll need all the knowledge I can get to live through this"

So I carried on.

"I had packed some clothes for myself and wrapped up little Kathrin.
We then went outside and met with the stranger. He looked at us then turned away.

"Follow me" he said
"Sir, what's your name?" I asked him.
"Gabriel Van Helsing; and your name young man?" he responded.
"Jedediah Smith Sir" I answered.
And so began my new life.
Many years had passed since that tragic evening.
I was now 17 years of age and my young sister was 8. Gabriel had taken such good care of us, and through those eight years; he had been training me.

I had learned a great deal about these Vampires, I had learned of their history as well as their strengths and weaknesses.
It was said that they had descended from the Devil and were his children. They took the form of humans but drank the blood of living humans to survive. They also have other weaknesses; such as, sunlight, holy water and crucifix of the Lord, as well as steaks through their heart, which would kill them in an instant.

It was fascinating, and I took nothing but pleasure in knowing the weaknesses of the Demonic creatures that killed my parents"

I stopped for a moment and re-read the weaknesses.
"Well I can say that I knew most of that, partly because of the weird Vampire movies in the media nowadays" I said to myself.
I then decided to read a bit more before soon settling into bed.

"Gabriel had been like a father to me all these years; he fed us, clothed us and protected us.
Kathrin had learned how to form weapons with the other women in the village that we had moved to miles from our old home.

It was similar to my old Village but a bit bigger, and more dangerous.

There were many Vampires that lived here and they enjoyed killing all humans they could find.
Leaving the village was too dangerous, as well as everyone not wanting to leave.
They claim Vampires invaded the country and they wouldn't leave unless all Vampires were dead.
So they stay and fight until they were no longer festering their home"

"I can honestly say, I know how he feels" I commented before I carried on reading.

"It's my birthday today, 13th June, I am now 18.
On special occasions like this we would celebrate in the Village church where we won't have any killing attempts.
It was a beautiful day and for the first time in months we actually had sun in the day time, instead of being shrouded in darkness.
So we were able to celebrate part of my birthday in the wonder of the sun.

The morning was full of fun and laughter, all the children played with each other; the women made large amounts of food and the men talking and laughing together.
It was indeed a wonderful day for me, and it got even better when Gabriel gave me my gift, he had given me a black crucifix that was lined with silver and had rubies placed at each point and a large one in the middle.
He told me it had been a gift from his father to him, and because he had no sons he passed it to me"

At the end of that sentence I stopped and felt for my cross around my neck, it was the exact same one Jedediah was speaking about.
"T...this belonged to him" I stuttered as I sat up and pulled the book closer to me and carried on reading once more.

"I couldn't be more honoured to receive such a gift from him, then again; it would be the last gift I would get from him.

It was the next evening now, and we were all packing things away from training and weapon creating. The sun had been shining here and there that day so those Vampires were not stalking the villagers.
But night had fallen quite fast and the darkness was indeed gloomy that night.
We all settled into our homes early that evening, not forgetting to sprinkle holy water around our doors and hang crosses from the door frames.

Kathrin and I were sharing a room together for the time being, and by the time of midnight we were both sound asleep. But for some reason I felt a disturbance and I awoke and sat in bed as sweat ran down my face.

I wiped myself and then sat on the edge of my bed; I then thought to
check on my sister.
To my horror, she wasn't there.
Instead of startling Gabriel I quickly put some shoes on and grabbed my
cross he had given me and quietly looked around the house, but sadly I
could not see her anywhere; living room, kitchen, bathroom nowhere, so
made my way outside.
Despite the darkness, I couldn't see anyone around. So I continued into
the village, still nothing or no one could be seen.

I sighed as I stood against the large oak tree in the village centre; I
relaxed myself before thinking about what I should do and where I should
look for her.

Strangely I think I began to hear laughing. I stopped breathing just so I
could hear where it was coming from; the forest. With that I followed the
sound and kept hiding behind trees as I went further in so as no one
would see me.

"Please you can't catch me by doing that Ryan" said a familiar voice, my
sister's voice.

I slowly peered around from the tree I was behind and saw my sister
running around with a boy around 11.
The only surprising thing was that I had never seen him before, but it
appeared that my sister knew him; as she called him by his first name.

"Oh please Miss Kathrin, you're just a bit faster than me" the boy said "

"Well this is interesting" I said to myself.
I then looked at the clock on my bedside table and saw it was indeed
getting late, but I had to keep reading just a little bit more.

"Miss Kathrin, can we sit and talk about what we were saying a few weeks
ago?" he said to my sister.

"Very well" she said as she sat under a large tree.
The boy then sat next to her; in the moon light I could see he had brown
hair and green eyes and fairly lighter skin than my sister. He was dressed
in what appeared to be a green shirt and long black pants.
"Why have I never seen this boy before?" I thought to myself.

"Now Miss Kathrin, would you ever consider joining my village; imagine
how fun it would be, we could play, laugh and banter like this all day and
night" he said as he rested a hand on her shoulder.

"Well I have thought about it, but I'd like my big brother to come too; he's the only family I have left" she said.

It was true that we never told Kathrin how our parents died, because she was still young and we were unsure if she was able to tolerate the truth; so we choose to say nothing.

"Come on Miss Kathrin, but just so you are aware our village goes through a procedure as to which you must 'change' in order to enter" he explained to her.

I have to say I didn't like what I was hearing; "change" what was the boy talking about?

"What do I need to 'change'?" my sister asked.
"Well it's quite like a transformation, or else we can't see each other, I'm sure you have noticed by now that I am unable to come out in the sun" he said

"I have noticed, why is that so?" she asked as she moved slightly away from him
"Well, Miss Kathrin, I'm not like the normal young lads you know; I am very different" he said as he moved closer to her.

Different indeed I thought to myself, this boy was a Vampire and he was trying to change my sister into one of his kind; well I don't intend on letting that happen.

"Step away from my little sister!" I called out as I stepped forward.
"Brother, what are you doing here?" she asked me.
"Kathrin, don't listen to that boy, he is a demon!" I shouted as I proceeded towards her.

"What are you speaking about?" she said as she stood up.
"Yes Sir, what?" said the boy who began to step back and stand behind Kathrin.

"You know what I mean you demonic sin of nature!" I exclaimed
"Brother please" she pleaded.
"Kathrin come with me now, we are going back home!" I shouted as I was getting closer to her.

I was suddenly pushed harshly to the ground and I scraped my knee and arm on the ground and drew blood.
"Damn it" I yelled aloud"

"Well this is getting more horrific than I would imagine" I said to myself before I carried on reading.

"She is not going with you young man" said a voice.
I looked up and saw a young girl standing over me around the age of 6 maybe 7.
"Who are you?" I asked as I stood up clearing the blood off me.
"My name is Mina, and we would quite like young Miss Kathrin to come with us, at least with us she can freely live without fear" she said as she smiled at me.

With the same horror I was stricken with all those years ago, I felt once again as I saw those animal like teeth in her mouth.

"Vampires" I said as I back away a few steps.
"Just let her go, besides she likes our company much more than yours" said the girl.

"No I'm not leaving without my sister!" I said as I tried to pass her.
"In which case, you won't leave at all!" she said as she grabbed my arm and threw me back into a tree.

She was strong; her physical strength was like nothing I had ever encountered. She stood before me and smiled once more, and I could see her features more clearly now. Raven black hair and sky blue eyes with light skin; strangely she was dressed in a pink and white Victorian dress that reached just above her ankles.

"Brother!" I heard Kathrin scream at me.
But that Ryan boy held her back from coming to my aid.
"Don't trouble yourself Kathrin, you are ours now" he said as he held her arms and rested his head on her shoulder.

"I'm sure because she's so young her blood will be fresh, but we shall not kill her dear boy, she'll forever be one of us; hiding in darkness and feasting upon the blood of her own previous kind" Mina said in an evil tone.

"Why are you doing this?" I demanded.
"You and your Gabriel Van Helsing should know that" you're the ones that killed our uncle!

"Yes, and I don't approve of that either" said Ryan, who still had a hold on my sister.

"You see Mina and I are siblings, 2 of 8 children, but thanks to your hunter our family is reduced" he explained

"But your uncle attacked my parents, now they are both dead!" I
responded in the same tone.

I then reached for my cross but before pulling it out I felt a slash across
my hand and it went flying away from me, I looked down and saw blood
leaking out from the wound. The girl had slashed at me quite badly.

"Ah, ah I think not; you will pay for what you have done my friend" she
said as she proceeded closer to me.

I suddenly heard her scream as I sudden whisk of wind slid past her face,
I look to the ground and saw a wooden arrow; then back to the girl and
saw she has a streak of blood upon her face.

"Who dares?!" she screamed
We all looked around and I saw from the shadows a familiar figure, it was
Gabriel.
"I dare, now step away from my family" he said as he readied to fire
again.

"Ah, it's you; the Vampire hunter, that's right my mother told me all
about you and your kind, killing us for a living" the boy slightly laughed.

"Well a little fact, we are not here alone" the girl slyly said.
But before Gabriel could say anything he was harshly shoved to the floor
from behind and the young girl rushed over at rapid speed and took his
weapon from him.

I then saw a tall man with black hair and green eyes standing on Gabriel's
back.
"Finally caught you Vampire Hunter" the man said.

The young boy shoved my sister aside and he and the young girl bent
down to Gabriel and took away all the extra weapons he had.
Kathrin had run over to me and protectively stood before me.
"Brother we should run" she said.
"No Kathrin, you run. Head back to the Village and get help, I shall help
Gabriel" I said.
Without arguing she did as she was told.

"Well the girl is no loss, we have an even better prize" said the man.
He then bent down and pulled up Gabriel's head up by his hair.
"I'll enjoy feasting on your blood" he said.
"You shall have a long wait monster!" Gabriel shouted as he managed to
reach for the vile of holy water he kept around his neck and threw it in his
face.

The creature hissed and pulled back and the children did the same,
Gabriel then ran to me and told me to go back to the village.
"I'm not leaving you alone!" I protested
"Jedediah please-"
"Look out!" I screamed as I pushed him aside and was forced against a
tree, staring into the eyes of that man.

"Leave him Medlock, that's enough. Just take your leave" Gabriel said as
he positioned a cross near the creature.

"I think not!" said a voice.
But by the time I saw who it was I heard a painful scream and turned to
see an arrow right though Gabriel's hand. He dropped the cross and fell to
his knees screaming.
I then saw the little girl had used his weapon against him.
Suddenly a gust of wind and the boy Ryan was at Gabriel's side.

"I can't wait to taste you, then my test will be over" he said
Without warning I saw the boy dig his animal like teeth into Gabriel's neck,
his screams were filled with anguish and it echoed all around the
surrounding forest.

I wailed in sorrow as I forcefully kicked the man away from me and
reached for my cross and held it to those demons.
They hissed and all backed away, the boy had let go of Gabriel and he fell
onto his front.
"Leave now!" I screamed.
They laughed as they disappeared into the darkness.

"Thank your sister for me, because without her; we never would have
completed our assigned task" I heard the boy laugh as his voice faded
away into the night.

I ran to Gabriel and turned him onto his back and saw his blood still
leaking out of his neck.
"Oh good Lord" I said as I tried to wake him up.
"Gabriel please, please wake up" I begged as tears began to fill my eyes.

Suddenly his eyes snapped opened and I gasped as I jumped slightly
back.

"A...are you alright?" I asked.
He stood up and moved his neck from side to side.
"Oh I couldn't be better my boy, but; I'm quite hungry" he then turned to
me and I could now see red glistening in his eyes.

"Oh no" I said as I stood up and began to back away.
"I didn't realise how much power one could have in this form" he said as
he stretched his arms.
"But enough idol talk, you're blood smells divine!" he said as he lunged at
me.
I rapidly moved aside and began to run away deeper into the forest. I
could hear him behind me which made me run faster, I knew not where I
was going but I had to get away from him.
Despite all my running I came to an end, I met with a mountain like wall
and had no way out.

"You're trapped boy" I heard a voice say.
I gasped as I saw him coming towards me with a hungry look in his eyes.
"Gabriel please!" I begged him.

He suddenly stopped and fell to his knees, tightly gripping onto his hair
and began screaming.

"Jedediah, please, please kill me! I don't want to live life like this!"
I cried at his words as I saw a sharp branch not far from me, I ran to it
and just as I turned to Gabriel he was already before me; his arms spread
out and he was going to jump upon me.

Out of fear I closed my eyes and pointed the branch in front of me. A
sudden jolt, followed by a horrific screams did I open my eyes and see
Gabriel over me, with the branch pierced through where his heart was.

"W...what have I done?" I said as I pulled away looking down at the blood
in my hands that had dripped down from his body onto the branch.
"T...thank you my boy, at...at least now I can rest in peace" he weakly
said as he fell to his knees.

"I don't regret taking you...o...or your sister in, look after her
Jedediah...s...she needs you" he said as he suddenly stopped talking and
fell onto his front forcing the branch further into himself.

I fell to my knees and cried in sorrow and pain. I had killed my friend and
my teacher that night. All because of those Vampires"

I stopped reading and closed the book.
Sighing I rested my head back and closed my eyes, as I did I felt tears
sliding down my face.
"These creatures have no mercy" I said to myself.
I opened my eyes again and with my sleeve cleaned my tears away.

"This cannot go on anymore, the existence of these creatures must end now; and despite the risks...I know I must be the one to do it, one way or another" I finally said.

I had made my choice, for the Pride of my Bloodline before me; I will put an end to these Vampires.

i want morebooks!

Buy your books fast and straightforward online - at one of world's fastest growing online book stores! Free-of-charge shipping and environmentally sound due to Print-on-Demand technologies.

Buy your books online at

www.get-morebooks.com

Kaufen Sie Ihre Bücher schnell und unkompliziert online – auf einer der am schnellsten wachsenden Buchhandelsplattformen weltweit! Versandkostenfrei und dank Print-On-Demand umwelt- und ressourcenschonend produziert.

Bücher schneller online kaufen

www.morebooks.de

VDM Verlagsservicegesellschaft mbH
Heinrich-Böcking-Str. 6-8   Telefon: +49 681 3720 174   info@vdm-vsg.de
D - 66121 Saarbrücken   Telefax: +49 681 3720 1749   www.vdm-vsg.de

Printed by Books on Demand GmbH, Norderstedt / Germany